ON MY WAY

ON MY WAY

Renuka Laungani 'Bharti'

ZORBA BOOKS

ZORBA BOOKS

Published by Zorba Books, April 2021

Website: www. zorbabooks.com
Email: info@zorbabooks.com

Cover design © Rishi
Copyright © Renuka Laungani 'Bharti'

Title : ON MY WAY

ISBN Print Book: 978-93-90640-35-5
ISBN eBook: 978-93-90640-04-1

Zorba Books Pvt. Ltd. (opc)
Sushant Arcade,
Next to Courtyard Marriot,
Sushant Lok 1, Gurgaon – 122009, India

"To all those souls who have done and are
doing good to humanity"

Acknowledgements

Zorba Books for publishing my second book

Preface

'On my way' is my second book containing short stories, the first being a novel 'Mehak- The fragrance' published through Zorba Books. The stories are based on true incidents with humour and pathos. Almost all the age groups can enjoy reading the stories which will touch their hearts as the incidents are those that take place in our daily life, but we do not bother to notice or pay heed to them. As human beings, understanding each other is of utmost important. The stories are based on our everyday experiences both humorous and pathetic, the characters are from middle class and lower middle class with fictional names.

Contents

CRABS ON THE PLATFORM

I t was 7am in the morning at western railway's Andheri station. Most of the Virar local trains halt at this station as it is one of the most important junctions en route to Churchgate.

The luggage compartment is normally always full with people carrying loads of different wares to be sold or handed over to the next person to be delivered elsewhere. At Andheri station, the local halts as it is a big junction where both fast as well as slow trains stop. People from Virar get down either to catch a slow local or to go to their destinations of workplace. Almost everyone is in a hurry either to get out or to get in the train as the halt is only for two minutes. Those two minutes are very important as one has to be very quick as well as alert or else it may cause not only delay in reaching their destinations but many risk factors can also be involved.

There are all kinds of vendors who carry their wares to different places to sell them, vegetables, fruits, fishes, milk, sweets, combs and what not being carried in baskets, cartons or polythene bags on their heads and shoulders are all in a hurry to get down therefore, they stand near the door, waiting anxiously for the train to stop.

It was Thursday. The Virar local was a bit late. People in the train as well as on the platform were waiting as usual very anxiously so that they could either be in or out of the train quickly.

No sooner the train arrived people from inside started pushing the ones in front to get down quickly. One of the fisher women, who had large size live crabs in her basket was pushed by someone from behind in such a way that all the crabs fell out of her basket on the platform as her basket tilted whilst getting down. It was a scene watching people running helter skelter seeing the crabs trying to run for their safety. There were people laughing and screaming passing all kinds of comments. It was very unfortunate that there was no camera man, no mobile phones at that time or else a video recording would have been a feast to the eyes and a good memorable film of a lifetime.

The fisherwoman was in a fit of anger seeing her loss for the day's earnings. There was not a single crab left in the basket, all were crawling in different directions to set themselves free from the maddening crowd and now that they had the opportunity, they ran for their lives. As the incident took place near the ladies compartment, most of the females dressed for their offices, waiting to board the same train could not get in due to the commotion and waited for the train to go so that they could catch the next train. They too, joined the crowd in the laughter, passing some comments and telling the fisherwoman to catch hold of the running crabs as soon as possible.

The young crowd especially the males whistled and hooted passing remarks such as-' See that big one he is going to Churchgate on his own, hahaha, when will he reach? Another said –Aunty that one is deserting you and going,catch him fast '. Meanwhile, the motorman too got down to join the fun and told the lady not to carry such huge crabs in the train. For a moment he too did not know what to do as one of the crabs had crawled down on the tracks which meant that if he started the train, the crab would die and the fisher woman would blame as well as claim from him the damages from the accident or the death of a crab which she had struggled so hard not only to catch but also to carry them all the way from Virar so carefully.

The train was delayed for about ten minutes. The people did not mind as it was a rare situation they were engulfed in. It was fun, an adventure which added some joy in their boring hectic routine travel. Many passengers got down to see what had happened and when they came to know the cause of the delay, they did not mind it because it had all set them rolling with laughter.

The fisherwoman was trying her best to catch the crabs that were nearby. No one else dared to touch the crabs, in fact they enjoyed watching them running away in all the directions and the people too trying to escape from them.

The fisherwoman started hurling abuses at the people laughing and commenting. Hers was an action worth noticing. She would run after one of the crabs, catch it and dump it in the basket closing with a heavy lid so that it would not escape again. She told the people to help her but no one ever dared doing so. Moreover, almost everyone is afraid of the these fisherwomen as they are not only terrible in their behaviour at times, but also because they do not think about the person opposite them and start not only uttering bad words but also because they know to teach any one a lesson of a life time. They start thrashing the person severely leaving him half dead therefore, no one has the courage to come in their way to save the sufferer.

Everyone keeps distance from all the fisherwomen and none can dare to tease, molest rape or harm them. Not only that, inspite of the amount of gold on their body nobody can rob them, pull their chains or even snatch them The lady could catch only two crabs and shut them in the basket. She said that she had eight huge ones and could not see where the others had slipped away when she was running behind the two to catch them.

The railway police arrived followed by two ticket checkers to inspect the cause of the delay and when they came to know about the unforeseen event, they smiled and decided to take the fisher woman to task and hold her responsible for the delay. The lady told how someone pushed her from behind due to which the basket tilted and all her crabs managed to be out of her basket which she had closed tightly with a heavy lid. She told that it was a huge loss to her and wanted the railways to compensate it. The ticket checker a clever guy, told her about the rules in return. He told her that she should show him nine tickets as each living being in the train should possess one be it a human being, a pet or any other creature for example the crabs.

Now this was a bit too much for the fisherwoman. She lost her temper, was out of her senses by this time, started cursing the people as well as the railway department. She said that she was being made a scapegoat in the matter for no reason and being punished for no fault of hers. She said that she was not the only one carrying live crabs every day, there were many others then, why should she be taxed and asked for so many tickets?

The ticket collector by this time was surrounded by crowds of passengers. He made signs to the motorman to go ahead and start the train adding that he would handle the matter. He told the railway police to summon the lady police on duty so that they could take the fisherwoman to their office and sort out the matter. The fisherwoman would not give in so easily. Some other ladies known to her now came to her rescue. They said that it wasn't any one's fault, that it was a rare situation and demanded more trains for that route and more compartments for luggage carriers thus changing the topic and coming forward to save their friend in trouble. They said that she was poor and lived with her only son who was all the time fishing in the deep seas.

The T.C. laughed and said that with half a kilo of the gold that she was wearing how could she be poor. The other ladies said that all of them wear that much or more gold which has come down from their ancestors.

The topic changed from crabs to whom did Mumbai belong because the actual and original residents of Mumbai were and are the fisher mongers whereas all the others have come from different corners of the country and the world who now dominate over them. The T. C. was at his wits end and demanded the tickets as soon as possible or the fine to be paid immediately as the ladies were just wasting everyone's precious time. Nobody seemed to budge from their stand. Meanwhile everyone forgot about the crabs gone astray but those who were eyeing them and were not in a hurry to rush to their offices kept track so that they could catch hold of them, so that a lavish dinner could be prepared and enjoyed by the members of the family.

The lady with two crabs informed the others that the railway board had corrupt officials and were trying to loot them by demanding heavy fine of three hundred rupees. She said she had only fifty rupees. The T.C.told the other ladies to help her with the fine as they had tried supporting her and were of the same community which was a bit too much for the ladies. They said that he should settle the matter with fifty rupees and give the receipt for the same or else they would complain that he had swallowed the money. But he said that if he had to give them the receipt, they would have to pay the full amount as he had to mention all the details in it or else they should all spend three days in the police custody. Hearing this the women removed their sharp sickle like cutters used for chopping fish and started threatening the men saying that they would not spare them. They said that the men were taking advantage of the ladies.

The women created a lot of chaos abusing and muttering all sorts of words that came out of their mouths without thinking. People getting in and out of the train were all collecting to see what was going on. Without understanding the matter, the men requested the T.C. to leave the women alone and not to mess with them. But by this time it became a matter of pride for both the sides to give up. The women said that they would not give in so easily and demanded the railway police to write a report about the character of the T.C. who wanted to tease and make fun of them. They told that he should be removed from his post as he was allowing all the ticketless passengers to escape and bent on merely harassing the women.

Many trains got delayed as passengers as well as the motormen stopped to peep in wanting to know the seriousness of the matter. Some walked away, whilst others joined the crowd trying to give their own suggestions. Finally, the senior supervisor walked in and said that they should sort out the matter in his cabin. So, the entire group started heading towards the cabin. Meanwhile, the lady with the crabs quietly slipped away and was out of the station area quickly slipping out from a narrow passage. She had taken advantage of the crowd as she was on the other side. She pretended that people were pushing her again and wanted to be in the safer zone but it was her own idea of escaping as she was fed up with the unnecessary argument.

When the crowd reached the supervisor's cabin, the discussion started all over again. The supervisor started explaining the rules all over again to which the ladies replied that they knew them. The fact was that in all the mess, nobody noticed the lady with the crabs move aside a little as the people were multiplying to see what the matter was. There was an additional crowd after each train that stopped at the platform. She was clever enough and managed to brush aside and walk out of the platform through a small outlet, took an auto and disappeared quickly.

The crowd started shouting whereas the station master along with the railway police tried to control and calm them. He took out the receipt book and asked to deposit the fine but when he tried to hand over the slip for money, the lady was nowhere to be seen. He shouted at the crowd and told them to move aside to give way to the fisherwoman so that she could come forward. The other fisherwomen turned around to see where the lady was and not being able to notice her, realised what had happened. They said that they were wasting their own time and one by one came out of the cabin saying why should they bother as it was not their matter and no way connected to the lady. The railway police too was shocked and blamed the crowd for unnecessary interfering in someone else's matter thereby giving her a chance of escaping.

The lady had however learnt a lesson and went away swearing that henceforth she would always buy the tickets for the live crabs and would never get down at Andheri station in future.

STRANGERS AT HOME, FRIENDS ABROAD

Two families who were staying in the same society named Royal Plaza hardly had any intimate relationship with each other as they stayed in different wings of the same building. The elders of the Kulkarni and Patil families met like others only on occasions like the general meetings, weddings, birthdays or on specific occasions celebrated by the public in general.

Nothing unusual at all in modern housing complexes as each one is busy in different ways of earning pertaining to different sectors. All the educated lot kept themselves occupied in their personal matters and hardly bothered to interfere with the lives of others. Whenever the forty eight heads of families met, it was a discussion on the welfare of the society and some general talks about the members of their families.. Apart from that, the children played and became intimate friends due to their interests in their specific games or chats.

It was a cosmopolitan society wherein all the festivals were celebrated with great fervour in which people participated enthusiastically. Otherwise, it was just a peaceful place without anything happening in particular. The female members were all working women trying hard to add to the income of their families. It was a cosmopolitan middle class society.They met in a hurry either in the lift or staircase on their way to and fro greeting each other inquiring about the wellbeing of their families in short conversations.

It was during the rainy seasons that people very often wished for a holiday to be at home, enjoy steaming hot snacks with tea or coffee and chit chat with the loved ones, relaxing, watching the pittter-patter of the rain drops falling below, soaking the parched earth deeply. The overflowing water formed little streams and rushed towards the sloping areas, finding space by itself to mingle with the waters gushing towards the rivers or the sea. The younger crowd normally preferred getting drenched, not minding about the consequences of the weather conditions. Children did not bother about the warnings of their parents and often sneaked out without their notice in the rain specially when it was a holiday only to return sneezing, muddy and fully drenched after enjoying an hour or so in the cool weather.

One such rainy day, there was a sudden outbreak of bacterial infection in various places. In almost every household, there was someone or the other suffering from some kind of health problems. Doctors had a hectic time treating numerous patients streamlining at their clinics. The sons of both the Kulkarni and the Patil families named Suhas and Harsh both studying in grade seven, were seen at Doctor Gokhale's clinic with their mothers waiting for their turn to see the doctor. The mothers recognised each other so did the children but excepting for the exchange of smiles not a word was spoken. After some time, Suhas broke the ice. "No school today but we cannot do anything else except take the medicine and stay in bed."

"I will come in the evening to your house. We will play cards" Harsh replied. His mother was furious." Nothing doing, as it is I had to take leave from office due to your health. You children do not even listen and run about in the rain eating the rubbish outside. Home- made food is not at all appreciated. Sit in the house with your books and finish your home-work."

"True, these children do not even listen nowadays. I had to attend an important meeting but now I am here waiting for our turn. It is taking so long. These men leave all the responsibility on us. We have to do three times the work of men and still be called the weaker sex. House work, office work and take care of the children too after delivering them." Mrs Kulkarni seemed to be quite frustrated and looked angrily at her son. The children felt guilty and remained quiet for sometime. When their turns came, they were checked by the doctor, took the medicine and went home quietly. It was the end of the conversation for the day.

Years rolled on, parents busy in bringing up the children, taking care of their education and doing their duties in making their living better and happier. It was time to decide about choosing a particular course, the need of right direction to fulfil the ambition so that the future could be rightly channelized. Normally, children love to imitate not their parents but their friends when it comes to the question of their higher studies. It is the age where the mind is more open to the suggestions and influence of the friends than to those of the parents Friends prove to be more important than anyone else therefore most of the styles, thoughts and the future course of action are often based in accordance to them. Suhas Kulkarni wanted to become a mechanical engineer like one of his senior friends, Mehul, and so took admission in the same college. On the other hand, Harsh too, following one of his friend's advice, joined a college for a course in computer software. Both the friends forgot about each other as they had a new friend circle to move around with.

It was time to come to grips when both were in their final year of their respective courses and had to decide about their future by joining a company either for earning or specialising in their fields. The Kulkarni family had three more daughters and had a tough time in educating the children. They decided to send Suhas abroad for a suitable job so that they could be in a better position financially. Marriage of their daughters in good families was also their prime concern. Hence, they needed a lot of money. Suhas started hunting for job opportunities abroad and was lucky enough to get one in the Middle East. He had got an opportunity of serving in a reputed company as a supervisor with a good package. What else does one want? A free quarter for staying, good perks,along with good food service.

On the other hand, Harsh who had completed his software engineering, was selected in an open campus interview as the manager of a well known firm on his merit. His parents were overwhelmed seeing the appointment letter offering him the best package they had never in dreamt of. It was like a celebration in the family with the whole house rejoicing at the prospects of good future not only for Harsh but for each one as all their problems could be solved easily.

Harsh too had got a job in the middle East but was unaware that Suhas was also working in another firm in the vicinity. They both started their jobs with eagerness. A year passed by but still they did not get an opportunity to meet or come to know about each other's where abouts nor did their family members meet or discuss about their sons in the society. The two families shifted to different places buying bigger apartments in the suburbs of the city as their financial conditions had improved to a certain extent. The company in which Suhas worked grew with a turnover of crores double than the previous year all because of his killer attitude of pushing the company's assets to a greater extent. The outcome of the results pleased the owner which made him extremely happy and sent Suhas to United States to open another branch. The excitement of a promotion and being sent to another country was immense thus making Suhas work harder than ever.

California proved to be very lucky for Suhas. He not only got a promotion according to international standards but name and fame making his parents proud. Harsh changed his job and went to California for better prospects grabbing the opportunity as it came along. Here, both Suhas and Harsh happened to settle down in the same locality though worked in different organisations in the neighbourhood.

Back in India, through communication, the parents as well as their sons were astonished to learn that they were so close to each other although they had never met. Phone numbers were exchanged and on one particular weekend, they arranged a meeting cum outing. A strong bond was established between them. Whenever they met, it was a like a celebration of memories, people, their jobs, relatives, future plans and happy times. As time passed by, the two of them became very friendly to the extent that they started sharing every little detail between them as well as their families.

Now, Suhas had a younger sister who too like him wanted to join him abroad. She too worked hard in order that that she could get a chance to join her brother. But her parents had other plans for her. They wanted to get her married soon as they had found a suitable match for her in Sholapur which she was not in favour of. Shivani had her own plans. She too wanted to go abroad and disclosed the matter to her brother who promised to support her.

After her twelfth, she decided to go for higher studies in the medical field and succeeded in getting through all the necessary tests required for admission in a foreign university

All going well, the three of them now stayed like family members getting to gether on various occasions.Shivani soon fell in love with Harsh and they decided to get married. When the parents learnt about it, there was no opposition whatsoever and agreed to go ahead with the children's plans. It was celebration time in their residential complex. They had never dreamt of such happenings because people hardly ever come so close staying in the same locality.

Now, there were many girls eyeing Suhas from the same complex but he didn't bother to mingle with anyone as he had already set his heart on an Indian working as a colleague with him. But he was happy for his sister.

People who never bothered even to look at each other due to busy life or rather not having even the slightest interest in each other at home, become so intimate abroad that even marriages can take place between them. One realises the value of togetherness with your own people only when you either miss them or when you are amidst foreigners. The urge for belonging to your own country and love for it is intense when you are away from your country.

77, BEACH VILLA

I t was known as a haunted bungalow although no one spoke much about it. A huge mansion with garden all around and a lovely beach in front where the fishermen, after catching variety of fish, sold them in different markets of the city. There were a few cottages too around the bungalow where most of the people of different communities stayed.

The bungalow was occupied by a family whose head was a strong and a bold woman.She had rented many of the rooms of the bungalow to some of the tenants as they were vacant in the spacious bungalow.

A police chowki consisting of just one room with a phone was just adjacent to the bungalow. One or two policemen were seen during the day time but night no one even had the courage to remain present in the premises. The phone kept on ringing many times during the night but there was no one to receive the calls. This was the place which was haunted and therefore 77, Beach Villa got its name as Bhoot Bungla.

As children, we never saw anything but staying inside the bungalow which had a huge compound with all the kinds of trees and the loneliness around were scared at times, hearing horrifying stories from others. Parts of the bungalow were slowly being rented out as it lay vacant because the landlady did not show any interest in staying there. She had another huge house elsewhere in the city. Most of the time the main part of bungalow was locked but there were servants who looked after it as well as the garden.

There were snakes too, green ones as well as the black ones due to the thickness of trees, the grassy lawns and a variety of fragrant flower trees which made the place look like a paradise. The snakes never ever harmed anyone. There was a palm tree near the entrance of the gate and very close to the police chowki. Instructions were given to the servants to light an incense stick on this tree. Trees are worshipped according to Hindu religion everybody knows but no one ever heard of a palm tree being worshipped.

When asked, the servant replied that there was some spirit in the tree and whosoever urinated near it became dumb due to his tongue being swollen like a huge ball in the mouth..Those that suffered had to beg forgiveness from the tree and they started lighting the incense sticks in the evenings after sunset. They became all right after sometime learning a lesson of a lifetime.

During night time whoever passed the police chowki after midnight, could hear some cries of small infants crying or laughing from inside. This was the incident that frightened even the policemen. No sooner it was eight in the night, they left the place after locking it and returned only the next day. When the new inspector took over the charge, he felt it was just some kind of a prank or superstition and decided to investigate the entire incident himself saying that he did not believe in ghosts or spirits either good or bad. One particular night, he came with a few of his office staff members to see for himself as to what was inside it in the night. Before he could open the door, a large number of people assembled there as they had heard about the new daring inspector's plans. Each one was excited to see the future course of events.

They heard the sounds of small babies laughing as if somebody was trying to tickle them or play with them. At first, they decided to see from the ventilator as to who was there. They had already kept some of the equipment ready for the fear of facing some unknown facts. The inspector stood on a stool and saw four beautiful crawling babies playing and moving about happily. There was a shock on his face. Soon the others climbed one by one and were shocked too wondering how the babies got in the locked place with not a single adult member inside it. They told that it was better to leave the place and to run for their safety.

But the inspector did not want to give in. He said that he had come to solve the matter as that was his duty and would remove the babies from the place. People told him not to open the door and take any action as his life would be in danger but the inspector would not budge from his decision. He opened the door and walked inside, the others looking with fright. The babies did not have any effect of his entrance, nor did they bother to look at him and continued their laughter in their usual way.

This annoyed the inspector all the more. He caught hold of one of the legs of a baby and walked out so as to drag the baby in such a way as if he was throwing the baby out of the room. He felt the weight a bit too much but continued walking out on the road. His intention was to drop the baby at the turn of the road and not look back. So he did, trying to drag the heavy load wondering how a small child could be that heavy and left it at the turning. But he wanted to see as to what was it that he left on the road. He turned to see and was utterly shocked. What he saw was absolutely nothing, then what was he carrying for such a long time?

He went home sweating due to fright and the next morning people understood everything when they did not even want to attend his funeral. They just saw it from safe distance.

The next strange episode which we children witnessed was that of the snake charmer. The bungalow at that time was being taken care of one Mr. Hamid who wanted to get rid of numerous snakes in the garden. He contacted a snake charmer who promised to catch the snakes if he paid him fifty rupees per snake as it was a very difficult task to call the snakes from the huge greenery. After a lot of negotiations twenty rupees per snake was settled upon. Now this caretaker, Hamid knew certain tricks and felt the snake charmer may not do the job well and would run away with the money without catching a single snake.

Street performers knew some ways of hypnotising the onlookers. Black magic and chanting of some unusual words was what was in vogue in fifties and sixties. It could also be the illiteracy, ignorance and superstitious beliefs of those times. The snake charmer started blowing the Pungi or the bean to attract the snakes. It was a lovely filmy tune and what we as children saw was that one by one two snakes came from the garden side and entered straight into his basket, curled themselves and put their hoods down.

He was about to get up after shutting the basket when Hamid suddenly shouted, 'cheat, rogue' and started giving all the bad words he knew. He said that he saw the two snakes coming out from his basket, went round a little and entered the basket again. The snake charmer had understood that Hamid had been wearing the slippers in the opposite way which means the heel part was in front and the toe part behind. He wanted to run away but was caught red handed. Hamid later explained that by standing on slippers in such a fashion he could see the actual incident taking place.

There was a big fight and the snake charmer ultimately left without taking any money or catching the snakes muttering all kinds of bad words for the time that was wasted and the effort he had put in for blowing his lungs out in playing the pungi. Rare things happened and children flocked to places with amazement to catch a glimpse of the incident. A bungalow was to be constructed nearby on a vacant plot. When the ground was dug for the foundation, a huge circular construction was found below which must have been either a small lake or some other source of water dried up due to certain reasons.

The builder along with his team asked the workers to dig further down all around for the hope of finding some treasure. Meanwhile, the news spread about certain findings and the police came to enquire. Two stone pots were found with some silver ornaments in them which were confiscated by the police. Any such news made the children run to the site out of curiosity who made a big noise about it everywhere. A barrel filled with smuggled goods came floating near the shore from the deep sea. When the police came,they opened it and found it loaded with Swiss watches. The barrel was probably dropped from a ship when the smugglers felt that their secret was out and they would be caught. Those were the days when Indo-China and Indo-Pakistan war was going on and any kind of news created a flutter all around.

There was a case of seven ladies who got in a double dekker bus and tried to climb upstairs in haste though they were all pregnant. The conductor became suspicious and told the driver to take the bus to the police station. It was revealed that they were carrying liquor in tubes around their waist because there was prohibition of liquor during those days. Amusing incidents kept life going inspite of shortage of rations, kerosene and other supplies. Whatever it was, childhood days always remain fresh as if it had all occurred on the previous day.

THE TREASURE THAT NEVER WAS

Narsingh was poor and did not know what to do until he realised that he was good in bluffing people who readily believed in whatever he told them. Not only the illiterate but also the educated enjoyed his company because he could narrate any episode with such confidence and accuracy that people got swayed in his talks. He had the knack of attracting anyone towards him and whosoever met him spoke to him with love and kindness. He saw that even the lies he spoke was believed by many and so decided to become a fortune teller. After learning a little bit of palmistry and a few tricks in bluffing people, he decided to use a small little corner out side his house in some hours for fortune telling.

He started earning some money but since everyone knew him there, they did not even pay him much and got away by merely thanking him.

He decided to go to another town where people would be able to pay him more. He packed his belongings and set off to a town not very far off from his hometown. One common thing that he noticed was that people were more interested in acquiring wealth without working hard. It is a natural instinct to become rich quickly without any hard work. In fact that is the dream of practically all human beings.

He thought of a plan. He could get more money if he just pacified the people in some way or the other with his skill in assuring them about acquiring the wealth. He surveyed a particular area in a remote place far from the town and built up a story. He had some regular visitors who told him that they wanted money for their needs. Whatever they were earning was not sufficient.

Among the people who thronged his little place under the banyan tree were mostly the middle class as well as the poorest of the poor He decided not to cheat the poor but fool the middle class educated ones who did not want to work hard. There was a quack, an ayurvedic doctor whose business was not doing well, an educated youth who was jobless and did not want to continue farming which his father insisted upon, a clerk who worked in a small office who was poorly paid, a villager who just idled away his time talking about his woes and about two to three others who came to him quite often.

After he had surveyed the place, he told atleast seven of his customers separately that there was a huge rocklike stone under which there was a lot of treasure. Each one was told to keep it a secret and to go only in the middle of the night to dig the area, to collect whatever they could within three hours. He gave the same address to all the seven. Now all these seven people started planning individually with one or two of their faithful relatives to reach the spot and get the treasure. Narsingh had extracted a lot of money from each of the seven who readily gave him the amount he had asked for. After all they would be soon turning rich. Not only that, they were even willing to part with some amount of their booty as well and make him rich too.

The doctor,the clerk, the youth, the villager and others set out in the dark night very quietly along with one or two loyal relatives carrying spade and digging tools with them. Each one of them tried to catch a quiet route so that they would not be seen by anyone. The doctor took his assistant with him following some unknown route. The main road was not selected by anyone due to the fear of being noticed by anyone. As the youth was passing through one of the by pass lanes he felt he heard someone following him. Now the villager had also selected the same route but when he felt someone round he with his younger son quickly hid behind a bush. The doctor too did the same. The others too, taking a short cut or a longer one were all in a hurry to reach the spot as soon as possible.

All seven along with their near ones reached the same spot and were shocked to see each other with the excavating instruments. They started fighting as to who will dig first and collect the treasure. One of them said that they were wasting time and it was better that they should all dig and share the treasure. It was agreed upon and the digging went on for a long time. After lifting, shifting a huge stone from the place, they could not find anything when a small child suddenly said that they have been fooled and that they would get nothing. They started walking back with drooping faces tired and sleepy. They were so furious and ashamed at being fooled that instead of going home, they walkedstraight towards the house where Narsingh had put up.

They found the place locked because Narsingh had already fled from the place for another destination with the intention of making money from other groups who could easily be fooled by him this time by cooking up another story. The people who were cheated had no option but to keep quiet as the police would call them educated fools to believe in such nonsense of fake astrologers.

THE SPILT MILK

The local passenger trains in Mumbai have a luggage compartment in which people carry all kinds of stuff either to be sold, to be delivered to another destination or to be transported elsewhere. This being the easiest, cheapest and manageable mode of transport for the middle class and the lower middle class becomes hectic and difficult at times due to the overcrowded compartments. There are fights, arguments, jerks and pushes which cannot be avoided as each one tries to see their own convenience in order to reach their destination without any hassles. People get in or out at their fixed platforms and in spite of what happens inside the bogie, the train goes on at its speed picking and dropping thousands of passengers on the platforms of their choice.

On the platforms are crowds of people waiting for a particular train which they want to board in. The beggars approach the waiting crowd asking for alms. Some give them a coin or two so that they walk out from their sight whereas the others drive them away angrily in order to get rid of them.

An old beggar sat at the end of the platform looking hopefully at the people passing by. But nobody bothered even to look at him as they were all in a hurry to board the train and those that got down were in a haste to reach their working place. For some, stations are meeting places because they can have a quick necessary conversation or pass some parcel to be delivered elsewhere, so they keep sitting waiting for others.

People on the platforms are in their own world, talking on their mobiles, reading newspapers, magazines or looking aimlessly thinking of nobody knows what. Even though they see the beggars, they do not bother to think of them. Vendors, sometimes sell packets of chips, lozenges and other eats and many buy them but nobody bothered to give anything to the old man. He looked hungry and weak, he had probably not eaten anything for the past two days and seemed to have no strength to walk up to the people to beg. His feeble hands even shook when he put them forward to ask for alms but none of them cared to even look at him, they just passed by. Some instead of pitying him, got irritated saying that he was sitting on the way and told him to shift in some other corner.

All of a sudden, when a train arrived, people got down pushing each other in the crowd. A milkman carrying a huge container of about ten litres of milk was eventually pushed from behind by the crowd due to which the can tilted in a way that the entire milk got spilt on the platform. It was a huge loss for the milkman but nothing could be done. He abused the people whereas the others felt sorry for him. The beggar got up with some courage feeling it was a golden opportunity for him, went to the place and stooping like a monkey, started sipping the dirty milk from the platform. The others looked with astonishment and pity at the beggar who was busy sipping the milk.Some told him to stop but the man was so hungry and happy that he did not mind filling his stomach with the dirty, muddy milk.

It was probably the first time in his life that he had milk and seen so much of it. The dirt did not matter to him. It was his hunger that he wanted to satisfy, what went inside was not to be thought of at that moment. There was very little milk left in the can which the milkman gave it to the beggar in his bowl and told him to stop sipping the dirty milk. He felt happy doing so because somehow he would not get anything that day but had helped the beggar with his kindness. Soon came another train and the onlookers dispersed for their onward journey feeling sorry for the beggar.

THE DIAMOND EYES

Dacoits in central India were rampant during the pre Independence as well as the post Independence days. There were many reasons of some choosing the path of a dacoit. Looting the wealth of the rich was their main motive. The main reasons were revenge and poverty. There were many huge rocky hills in central India which provided safe hiding places for the dacoits and so it was very difficult to catch hold them. Moreover, the police too was at times afraid to oppose them due to the fear of revenge they might take.

The dacoits disguised themselves as villagers and went around surveying the area they wanted to loot or take revenge during daytime and then returned on horsebacks loaded with guns ransacking houses and punishing their enemies later in the night. As there were no banks in small towns those days, people hid their gold and money in some pots which were then buried under the ground which was later covered with mud or some stone. Whenever they needed it, they dug it open and made use of it. Such was the fear of the dacoits that even the younger girls were taken care of very strictly and not allowed to move out of the house even during daytime lest the dacoits would see them and kidnap them during the night. When the people heard the hooves of the horses, in the night, they were sure of some house being looted, some revenge being taken, someone being shot or killed at one go.

There was a famous temple of a deity in the town. The temple was very popular as people had complete faith in the goddess who answered most of their prayers. A lot of money was collected in the donation box. The trustee had asked the jeweller to make diamond eyes for the deity which was done so and the beautiful eyes were fixed in place of the stone eyes. The idol looked very beautiful and real with the shine in her glittering eyes. Whoever visited the temple, just sat there for some time staring at the deity as if being captured by her beauty especially by her diamond eyes. Day by day, the temple started becoming popular and people started thronging it in large numbers. The special prayers in the mornings and evenings were attended by large number of devotees who assembled there and returned home only after taking the Prasad.

The trustee was becoming richer due to the offerings by the devotees because whoever came definitely had something to donate in the box or to offer some sweetmeats to the priest to be distributed as the Prasad. Once, when the dacoits came to this town as farmers to make certain purchases, they heard about the temple and the deity's diamond eyes. They went to pay a visit and soon became greedy seeing the eyes of the deity. A wicked plan to steal the eyes as well as the donation box soon entered their minds. When they returned to their homes in the hideouts, they started planning about the way of plundering the wealth.

The same night they set out on horses to the temple. The priest was asleep in a small room behind in the temple complex. He was assigned the task of not only performing the rituals but also acting as the caretaker of the temple. Almost all the true devotees are afraid of doing any harm, robbing or cheating the sacred places no matter whichever religion they belong to. They are supposed to be the safest places as all religions preach about the fear and punishment God can give to the offender. The trustee was happy with the loyal priest and his duties.

It was a dark night although the dacoits had torches with them. They went straight to the deity and removed the eyes carefully. No sooner they turned their backs towards the deity to uproot the donation box and then to take it off, they turned blind. One of them screamed with fright saying he could not see anything. The other two said the same and could not even understand which way they should follow. Hearing the noise, the priest came out and asked what was the matter. He had understood that they were dacoits hearing the sound of the horses. The dacoits told him that they had turned blind. When asked what they had done, they told that they had removed the eyes of the deity.

The priest told them to ask forgiveness and to keep the eyes back which they did and no sooner the eyes were kept down, they could see again. They knelt low asking for forgiveness again and again. Not only that, whatever they had with them as booty, they placed all that in front of the Goddess, vowing that henceforth whatever they would steal, would be utilised only for the good of the poor. Thanking the humble priest, they went towards their horses waiting for them. The priest too, knelt and asked for forgiveness and the next day the eyes were replaced, after which the story was told to the devotees with a lot of pride about the deity's justice.

From then onwards, the temple became famous all the more and the priest would sing in praise of the deity some verses he had written himself in the presence of all the people who came there. The story has come down to the present generation from their ancestors. And the visitors who go to the town, do not fail to pay a visit to the temple and thank the Goddess who had taught a lesson not only to the dacoits but everyone that there is a superior power that keeps a watch on all our deeds and how one should lead a life of honesty, humanity and goodness. Whatever we do, we get the reward or the punishment accordingly.

THE TEACHER AND THE STUDENT

Ramila became a teacher after a lot of struggle in life. Her parents were poor and could not afford to send her to college. So she decided to give tuitions to small children and study on her own. She knew that only education would take her forward in life and this was the best option. Soon she was able to complete her graduation and complete her teacher's training. She was offered a job in a school which had changed to English medium from Gujerati medium as the demand for them was rising. It became a fashion to convert most of the vernacular medium schools to English medium as the admissions were dwindling and parents felt that students became more smart in learning all the subjects through English.

The school was in the initial stage of setting up in the new medium and within a month of announcement many students turned up for admissions. The management was very happy and kept admitting students without any hassles. Children of slums nearby, vendors, hawkers were extremely happy as the fees being less, provided a golden opportunity to study in English medium school. Now they could tell everyone with pride that their children studied English right up from the nursery level. New staff was appointed and Ramila was one of them. She too was happy to get a job very close to her house as she did not have to spend on travelling and could save some more time in studying further as well as in continuing giving tuitions.

The crowd that came was of the lower middle class society whose parents had never been to school or rather were not lucky enough to receive education. Hence the children were difficult to control and were very rowdy, stubborn and mischievous. Ramila was appointed as the class teacher of second standard. Due to the large number of admissions given, the seating arrangement became a problem either because of the small classrooms or due to shortage of benches in it. Three or four students sat on a single bench which became difficult for them to write and kept on fighting with each other. It was not teaching but only controlling the students all the time for the teachers.

Ultimately it was the teacher who had to face the management, parents and supervisor. Teaching was not possible and at the end of the day the teachers were tired shouting, controlling and maintaining order in the classes. They heaved a sigh of relief when they left the school premises. At the end of the year, some teachers left the job and joined other schools. Most of them were always on the lookout for better opportunities due to prevailing conditions in the school. Moreover, there were hardly any free periods due to the shortage of teachers. But Ramila continued and the management felt happy at it. She was also very polite and understood the situation.

The following year, she was made the class teacher of sixth standard which had the most notorious boys in the class. The others told her that she would have a tough time the whole year round because of Dilip in that class. This boy enjoyed irritating the teachers and did not allow the teachers to teach. Most of the time, he was punished either standing on the bench or outside the class. Wherever he was, he was a nuisance. When sent for his parents, his elder sister or father came, spoke to the principal or the teacher and went away saying that severe punishment should be given to Dilip. The supervisor on her rounds would often scold the teacher when she saw the class noisy.

Ramila was also fed up and did not understand how to control some of the boys because they would all join Dilip in the mischief. Once, the whole class was out for the P.T. period on the ground. The teacher told the boys to play quietly as she was not well and sat nearby on a stone bench. Ramila was in the staff room doing corrections. Dilip had some fight with Mangesh, who was the police inspector's son. Dilip, who was also known as a hooligan took the boys behind the school building and after stripping Mangesh, started boxing him. This was noticed by the supervisor from the second floor who came running down and went straight to the site where the boys were.

The P.T. teacher got a start on seeing her and followed her. She understood that there was some problem created by Dilip. The supervisor brought Dilip to the staff room and reported the matter to Ramila. At that moment what made her say gave a shock to Dilip. She said that she could not believe what the supervisor said because he was a nice boy. Actually she had noticed some innocence on his face and this time felt like taking his side. The supervisor was angry and told her that she would be reporting the matter to the principal when he came and soon there would be some police case as the inspector's son was beaten.

After the supervisor went, Dilip who was still standing there, did not know what to do. Ramila told him that he was her favourite student and she liked him. What made her say these words she could not understand. They just came out from her heart at the spur of the moment. She had never thought of them. These words melted Dilip's heart and he told her that he had done what the supervisor had said and added that on account of him she got the scolding from the supervisor. He was shocked how she had taken his side to save him from the untoward situation.

From the next day Ramila started giving importance to Dilip by making him do some work like minding the class, helping her in carrying the books and some errands which he enjoyed doing. He was ever ready to help the class teacher who felt so much for him and would ask her if she needed any help all the time. It was a turning point for both. Dilip did not have a mother so he stayed with his uncle and aunt who were all the time scolding and insulting him for his behaviour. His father remained out of the house most of the time, busy in various shooting locations working as a photographer. He did not get the mother's love therefore he had become a problem child. Children of split parents or single parent mostly are found to be problematic due to the lack of love.

He felt that someone understood him and liked him. A drastic change was seen in him. He started admiring Ramila, who treated him lovingly too, having realised the change not only in Dilip but also in her. She understood that such children did not improve by being punished but by being treated lovingly. Earlier, it was nothing but complaints to parents and different ways of punishments which did not help either the students nor the teachers. She used to get irritated and angry every now and then but realised that it did not work. It was also a lesson for her as to how such children should be treated. Dilip did well in the boards later and joined the navy securing a good position. He did not forget the teacher who had changed his life and made him a good human being. He would narrate several incidents of school life not forgetting to mention Ramila each time.

Ramila too, would not forget how she changed her method of dealing problematic children and would always mention to everyone about Dilip who was and would always be her favourite student, who had taught her to be a good and understanding teacher. Both had learnt a lesson from each other hence, it is truly said that life is nothing but giving and receiving which can be anything, anytime, anywhere.

THE ANCIENT GRAVEYARD

Matheran, a well known hill station, in the state of Maharashtra has been very popular since the time of the British. It is famous for some of the most important points worth visiting on horseback, going on long treks or hikes. Being the nearest hill station apart from Mahabaleshwar, Lonavala and Khandala for the people of Mumbai as well as Pune, it provides a suitable outing on weekends and holidays. Matheran has a cool pleasant climate, good budget hotels and scenic beauty. The toy train ride following the serpentine track from Karjat station to the top provides good view of natural beauty with greenery and red mud all around. It has maintained its peaceful atmosphere because no traffic is allowed inside the area. One has to either go on horseback or on foot.

A group of young college girls decided to go for a weekend and have some memorable time of their life. They had already booked a guesthouse which was far from the station but quite cheap which suited their budget. On their way they found that there were other hotels too which were vacant and cheaper as compared to the one they had booked. But as they had already paid the amount for the day they felt they should stay there and see the facilities it provided. The leader of the group said that they would change the hotel the next day if they found the present place not suitable. And so it did happen that the guesthouse they had booked was quite clumsy and crowded with public washrooms and long queues in waiting for their use.

The next day the group decided to change the hotel. The one they selected was totally empty having a huge open ground in front with a swing in it. Two rooms with three beds in each were allotted. There was open space all around it and both the rooms had separate entrance from outside as well as a door inside which connected both the rooms. The girls liked the place as they could be together in the night and have a nice time. The owner too was happy as he got customers who were all young girls and told them that whatever help was required, they would get it readily.

After keeping their luggage, the girls started going round the place thinking and planning about their stay for the next twenty four hours. As one of them went behind to observe the place, she came back screaming which gave everyone a shock as they could not understand what happened to her. She caught the hands of two girls and took them behind to see the place. The others followed them and everyone stood there for a while with open eyes. They saw an open graveyard which seemed to be unused for several decades. The whole place was covered with dried leaves and it was only because of the tombs that they could make out that it was a graveyard. From close distance they could read the names and the year of death of people whose bodies lay beneath them.

The years inscribed on the tombs were mostly those of the British period all before 1947. The girls read some of the names like John Crasto died on seventh March,1891 and so on. They went to the owner of the guesthouse and asked more about the place who told them there was no harm at all and that the place was quite safe. He added that till date no harm was done to anyone neither to him nor the guests, assuring the girls of all the assistance they needed. Now it was clear to the girls why the rates of the place were so less but as they had already made the payments, there was nothing they could do but stay there at least for twenty four hours. They decided to divide themselves into two groups and take their positions in the rooms.

The fear of some ghost appearing or some kind of evil happening was always there in their minds so they decided not to sleep and keep awake by having some fun. One of the groups decided to frighten the other group by playing some prank which was that a girl would go out quietly from one door and knock three times on the other door and come back quickly after closing it and pretend to be asleep on her bed. The knocking was to be in a particular fashion. When the knock was heard in the other room, the girls got a shock and started speaking in low voices that there was a knock and kept quiet for some time. After some time the girl who knocked went out again and repeated the knocking in the same fashion. Quickly back on her bed, everyone waited to see the reaction of the girls in the other room.

This time one of the bolder girls from the other room got up saying she would open the door and see who was outside but her partner screamed and told her not to open as it could be the ghost of uncle John. Then she said that she should see what the girls in the other room were doing, so, opening the middle door she peeped in and was a bit frightened to see that all were asleep with bedsheets on their faces. She went back and told her friends that the girls were all fast asleep whereas the girls were actually having a hearty laugh quietly. The next day it was time to leave the guesthouse and return by the toy train to the station. After packing, tea and breakfast was had without any talks because both the groups wanted to open the topic about the knocks heard in the night.

When the train started, one of the girls said that they had heard someone knocking their door twice in a particular fashion and they were sure that it must have been that of the ghost of uncle John. When the other group heard, they looked at each other but without any reaction on their faces as they knew it was their idea of frightening them.

It was on the way back home that one of them leaked out the secret plan about the plot of the night to frighten the girls of the other group. There were smiles all over and even the feeling of relief that they had left the guest house at last and the expression of confidence of doing something adventurous the next time.

CHEENIE, THE PARROT

For almost thirteen years, Cheenie, the cute little parrot had been my most loveable creature, dear to my heart, making me smile, laugh and cry whenever I think of her. It was difficult to do anything for her when she became old, to even feed her as she looked at me with almost tears in her eyes. Yes, tears which I could almost see as if to say that that I should do some thing for her to bring her back to normal life. But it was all over and finally during the wee hours of one morning, she died making everyone weep when she was buried in the backyard of the society complex.

Her whistles her squeaks and her shrill but sharp sounds stopped echoing making the whole neighbourhood feel the sorrow of silence in the atmosphere. Parting has always been sad, be it of anyone, as it becomes difficult to accept the loss specially of the one which is close to one's heart. Cheenie had become an important member of the family. She was given the freedom of being out of the cage for three hours daily during which she could fly to the window sill and look out at the scenery outside trying to speak certain words merrily. At sharp seven in the evening she would come down and hold my dress with her little red beak telling to put her back in the cage.

Every day at sharp seven, she would come down which often made me wonder about the time she would follow. I felt at times that it was darkness that made her come down as she could not get a proper view out of the window or could be that she was hungry as I did not give her anything to eat out of the cage or could have been that she was just tired walking to and fro on the window sill. Whatever could have been the reason, I felt happy at her behaviour that she followed a pattern which I too got accustomed to.

Another memory was that she whistled when she was happy and when a stranger came home. This act of hers made the stranger or the guest whistle too. If I sat beside her quietly watching the television, she would look at me squeaking loudly as if to say that I should talk to her and not sit in silence. Pudding and guavas were her favourite although she ate every thing that was given to her. She would make certain sounds happily to indicate that she enjoyed what was given to her. All the timings of hers were fixed. If we spoke loudly in the house to each other, she did not like it and would herself raise her voice as if to scold us in anger. Trying to shout at her was a kind of retaliation from her side as she rolled her eyes and looked at us in anger, shaking her little head and shouting at us angrily.

Once, during Diwali, a friend happened to come and sit by her side speaking to me. After some time, I brought sweets to offer my friend. No sooner my friend tried to take the first bite of the sweets, Cheenie screamed giving both of us a shock. Actually, she did not like the idea of my friend eating the sweets. It made us laugh making us realise that she should have been given to eat first or that an outsider should not eat in this house as he or she is not the member of the house like her. When I gave her to eat, she was happy.

Once a week she was given a shower bath after which she dried her wings and went immediately to sleep as she felt nice and cool. She appeared like a small child to me who came out after a bath happily cool and fresh. Every action and behaviour of hers was worth watching. One was never tired of her. If at all people spoke loudly or scolded her she would immediately retaliate by shouting back looking angrily, rolling her eyes at the person. Even when we spoke against her she would understand and shout in between as if to say that she knew what we were speaking about her.

A shower bath was her favourite which was given twice a week. Soon after the bath she would move around like a small child feeling fresh and cool. She dried herself fluttering her wings and each strand of her feather dried when she did so with her beak. Sometimes, she went to sleep even with the wet feathers due to the cool and fresh effect. That was her deepest slumber and she woke after half an hour feeling hungry which made her eat her food hurriedly.

Cheenie was so named because of her sweet whistle and the way she behaved with us like an obedient child. When the cage was kept outside for sometime, other parrots would come to her and then it was a real zoo like scene with numerous parrots opening their red beaks to speak to her at the top of their voices. When we sat watching the programmes on television, she too started looking in the same direction and watched what was going on. On certain occasions she reacted as if she was conversing with the characters on the TV. When I left the house for work she understood and kept watching quietly. On my return, she was very excited and fluttered her wings wanting me to sit by her side and talk to her. Whilst doing my work in the house, I kept on talking to her and she replied back indicating that she understood whatever I was saying.

Very often I would point out at her food in the cage saying,'See so much is there to eat. My Cheenie is hungry, eat this apple, eat this guava, eat the beans 'and so on. Believe me, she ate that happily. And every time she ate, she made such happy sounds indicating that she was enjoying it all. When the cage was kept outside, the other parrots came probably wondering why she was inside but were at the same time startled to see the amount of fruits and other eats given to her. So, I started giving them too which made only one of the parrots come closer to me and eat the beans from my hands. He would eat it merrily and fly away and then settled on the cable wire just opposite watching me and Cheenie.

Slowly, the friendship grew stronger and he started coming inside the kitchen and after eating whatever was given,I made him fly away as I didn't want him to move about anywhere in the house for the fear of any untoward happening as he was not trained. Sitting by her side and watching all the activities became a good pastime but when she grew old it was really painful to help her out. It was clear after thirteen long years that the time had come and any day she would die. It was time for her to say goodbye to us. We did whatever we could for her burial. Indeed, pets are such loving, adorable creatures!

POEMS

NATURE –A BLESSING

The long western stretch of the Arabian sea
Its waves towards the shores flowing with glee
The sun going down in it like a golden pot
The sky in the horizon behind looking hot
The birds flying across it towards their nest
It's time for all to end their work and rest
The moon appearing smilingly to peep at the earth
The day's work done folks, relax, it's your worth
The trees standing still with no breeze around
As if they are asleep too on the cool ground

The buds opening their petals slowly to bloom
Spreading joy and fragrance to banish the gloom
The hills in the East through which the sun rises
Playing hide and seek through clouds of all sizes
You have blessed us with a wonderful nature, Oh! Lord
Humans, use it wisely and thank the God!

CHILDHOOD

Going to school eating chocolates on the way
Returning home merrily at the end of the day

Throwing away the bags, books and shoes
Now is the time for play and no more 'do's

Let people howl, shout or anything say
We will play and enjoy, come what may

Parks and grounds with children around
Shrieks of laughter and joyance abound

children with smiles and clothes so colourful
making the atmosphere more pleasant and joyful

Vacations were planned to be spent in various ways
Adventures, visits and eatables on all the days

Leaving no room for loneliness, boredom or homework
As that would spoil the holiday or only irk

Visits to grand parents were full of gifts, love and care
They never failed to fulfil our wants and tried to share

Whatever they had and could for their loved ones
For their children, daughter in laws or grandsons

Evenings spent at beaches, monuments and different places
Historical tours, various cultures, dresses and pretty faces

Purchases from amount saved in piggy bank
Spending it made everyone more happy, bold and frank

There was always an urge to find some hidden treasure
Trips to ruins and rare places became a fulltime leisure

At the end of vacation, everyone turned very sad
Going back to school, the very thought was bad

Memories of friends, foes, joys, sorrow or fun
In weathers of rain, snow, storm or under the sun

Will remain immortal till the end of our lives
Whether stored in our memories or in the pendrives

IMPRINTS

People, Situations, Dreams and Nature
Flash one by one in my mind
With images of their first imprints
And messages of all kind

The stern faced Irish nun with all her strictness
Staring at us with her warning finger
When we played mischief, remained absent
Or tried anywhere to linger

A principal of rare qualities was she
No doubt, trying to see us through and through
From her glassy eyes, brown tunic, stiff looks
And the sparkle from her eyes so blue

A friend so rare, never a critic
Full of encouragement, praises and advice
When I stood motionless on the stage
Or looks not really very nice

My dance was superb, was her reply
You were cute, smart and indeed the best
I wondered whether it was a pun or a joke
To think that I was better than the rest

A swing of roses in a dream I saw
Swaying on it merrily, high and low
At the age of five was a memorable scene
No sorrow, no tension, just love, no woe

These were the lessons of a lifetime
That life is a blend of both joy and sorrow
Ups and downs will always be there
Be it yesterday, today or tomorrow

In my teens, went for a trek to the mountains
Trying very hard to reach the top
Time and again took a pause to relax
To see our calories burn or the sweat drop

What is it that keeps us going in life
In taking risky steps to go against the flow
Admiring nature that gives us all the happiness
Being determined is the key even if you are slow

Finally, it is the power above who gives us the strength
So, accept whatever He gives and never mind
Because in them are the riches many
And the treasures of all kind

MUMBAI CITY

From –Bombaim to- Bombay to- Mumbai like a roller coaster
A mere change in the names and a bit of a tongue twister

For every ruler and government tried to do something new
And doing so they changed the history of the place too

After doing some research, each had his own say
The renaming should be done come what may

And, on the pretext of doing so the city wore a new look
But in saying 'Mumbai' some time it surely took

Predictions, articles, discussions were all turned down
Who cares whether people like it, smile or frown?

The goddess Mumbadevi has at last got her dues
She will now figure and be remembered in the news

Both the haves and have nots live here side by side
Some who lead the people astray, some who rightly guide

A never ending existence of a wild goose chase
For everyone wishes to be ahead in the race

A choice one can have from a number of streams
Or leave it to the others to fulfil their dreams

All types of people in this city can easily be found
Living in the skyscrapers or on the plain ground

There is money, glamour, fame and assurance
Whatever you desire is available in abundance

Nobody cares whichever way you choose to live
There is no time whether you commmit crimes or forgive

There is always something or the other happening
Which can be exciting, shameful, funny or sickening

Each gets involved by becoming a part of it
Contributing whichever way one feels fit

Mumbai is indeed a city very unique and loveable
Whatever it offers is always nice and adorable

LIGHT OF HOPE

The virus that has taken the world in its stride
Without weapons, words or hatred far and wide

Has brought down the economy and man to the grave
Left with warriors to fight and living beings to save

These angels in white with their patience and skill
Doctors, nurses and medical staff with their mighty will

Treating the patients no matter who they are
Though they have pelted stones on them to keep them afar

The policemen controlling the unruly mobs everywhere around
Doing their duty amidst the crowds that abound

Taking the law into their hands to show their uncivilised strength in turn
The tables soon turned around for them becoming a lesson to learn.

Warriors are the people with their strong commitments
Keeping the situation under control in all the segments

Many who were infected too and passed away
Doing their duty whilst keeping their families at bay

These angels should be respected and given support by us
Salute them, co-operate with them without any frown or fuss

Pray for their well-being and help them thrive
May God teach everyone to love, unite and strive

In creating a world of compassion and oneness
Showering hope, love, blessings and togetherness.